Quack, Daisy, QUACK!

JANE SIMMONS

Little, Brown and Company
Boston New York London

To Ruby and Denis, who never shout

First U.S. Edition
First published in Great Britain in 2002 by Orchard Books

ISBN 0-316-79587-9
LCCN 2001092435

10 9 8 7 6 5 4 3 2 1

Printed in Singapore

Daisy and Pip loved visiting Aunt Lily's.
There was always so much to play with.

There were the flowers.
"Buzz!" said Daisy,
"Buzz!" said Pip,
but the bees flew away.

Everyone was quacking and it was so loud.
"Now you can make as much
noise as you like!" said Aunt Lily.

"Come on," said Aunt Lily,
"I know a perfect place for
being noisy!" and they all set off.

And there was the bird feeder.
"Tweet!" said Daisy,
"Tweet!" said Pip, but
the birds took off too.
"Oh dear," said Aunt Lily.
"Try being a bit quieter," said Mama Duck.

Daisy and Pip tried, but
they were too excited,

eek

eek

and the mice ran away . . .

splish

splosh

and the fish
went too . . .

and even the balloon
floated up, up, and away.

bang

bang

Then there was
nothing to play with.

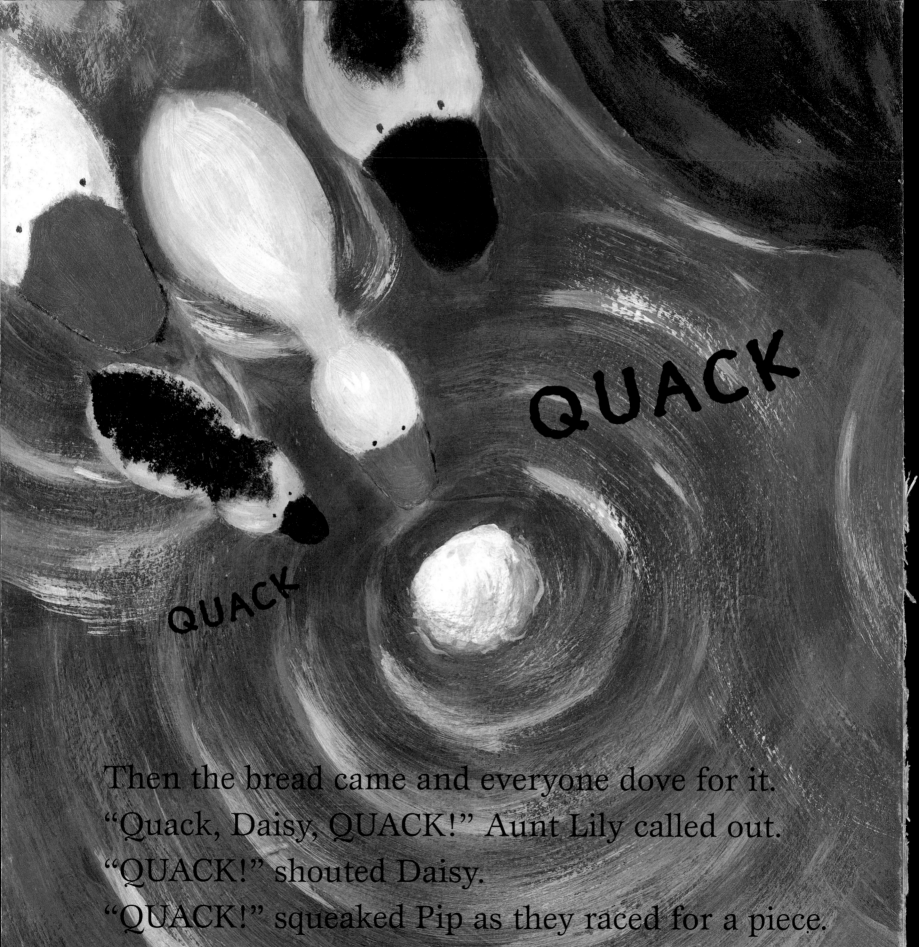

QUACK

QUACK

Then the bread came and everyone dove for it.
"Quack, Daisy, QUACK!" Aunt Lily called out.
"QUACK!" shouted Daisy.
"QUACK!" squeaked Pip as they raced for a piece.

They got it,

and pulled

and pulled

until it broke in two.

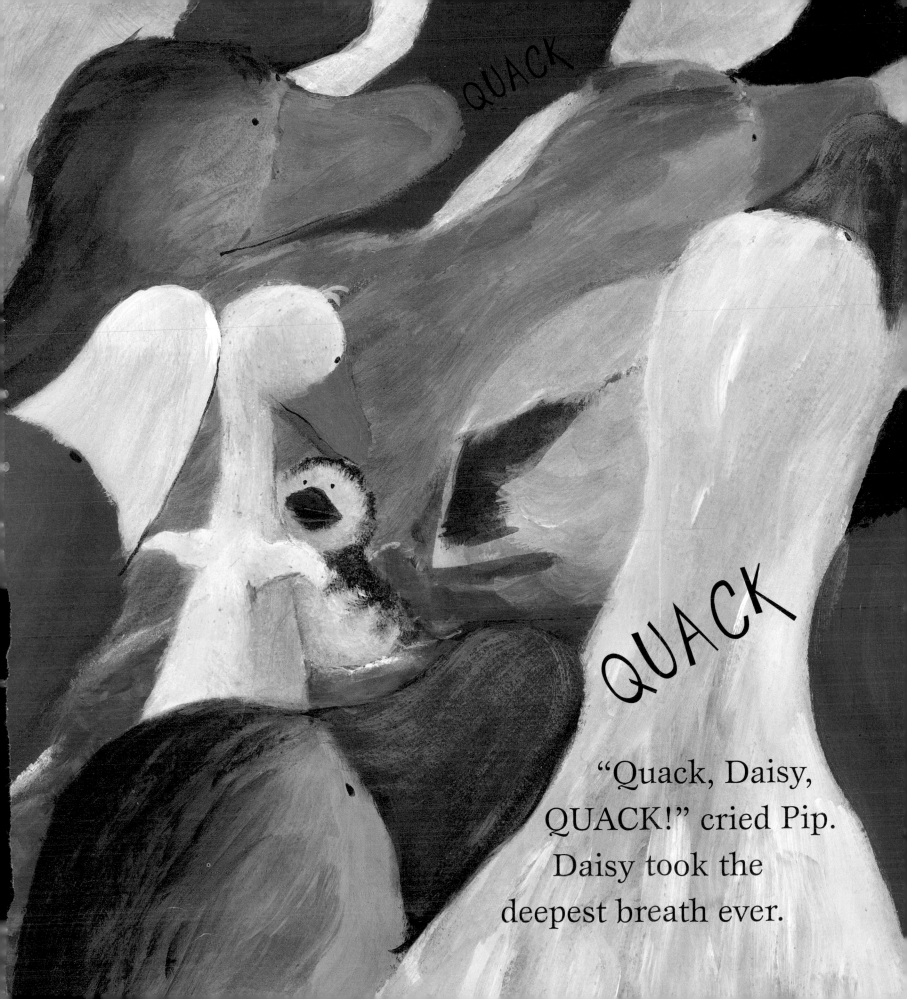

QUACK

QUACK

"Quack, Daisy,
QUACK!" cried Pip.
Daisy took the
deepest breath ever.

Everything went quiet.

Then they
softened it

and munched
it down.

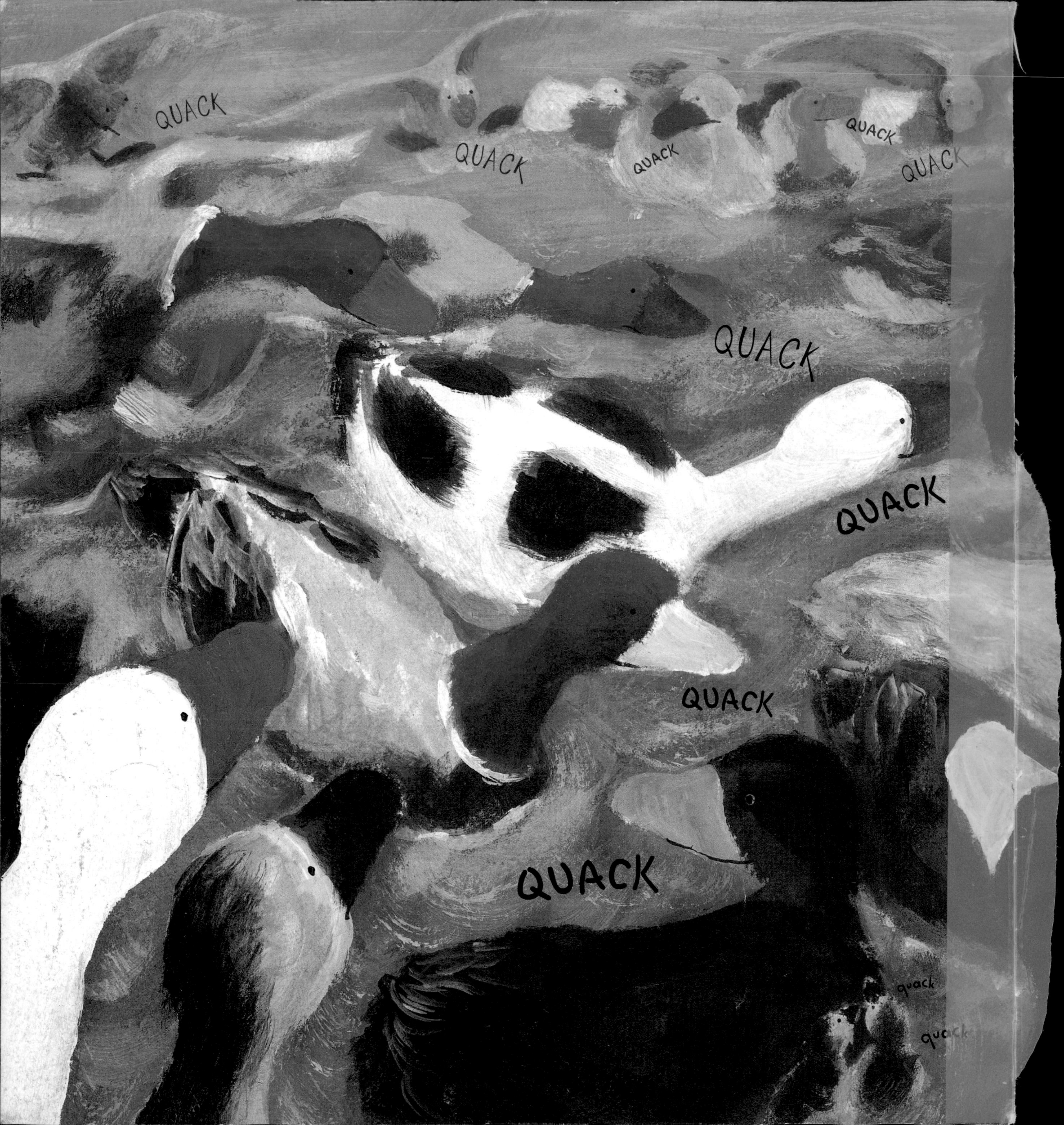
QUACK
QUACK
QUACK
QUACK
QUACK
QUACK
QUACK
QUACK
QUACK
quack
quack

Suddenly there were ducks
everywhere, and everyone was quacking!
"Daisy! Pip!" shouted Mama
as they disappeared.

QUACK

QUACK

Daisy couldn't see Mama or
Aunt Lily anywhere.
"Where's Mama?" cried Pip.

QUACK

But all the quacking was too loud.

"Mama!" cried Pip. "She can't hear us," said Daisy.

QUACK

QUACK

More bread
came and
everyone was
pushing and
shoving and shouting.

QUACK